HAVING IT ALL

▼▼▼▼▼▼▼▼▼▼▼▼

COMING TO AMERICA
FROM MEXICO–1920

M. J. COSSON

COVER-TO-COVER BOOKS

Chapter 2

Perfection Learning®

Cover Design: Tobi Cunningham
Inside Illustration: Margaret Sanfilippo is of El
        Salvadorian and Italian descent and now resides in
        Greenbrae, California.

Cover Image Credit: Digital Stock

Acknowledgments

Many thanks to Lillie Martinez, James and
Suzanne Meehan, and Lupe Ruiz-Flores for
your thoughtful review of this story.

Printed in the United States of America.
For information, contact
Perfection Learning® Corporation,
1000 North Second Avenue,
P.O. Box 500,
Logan, Iowa 51546-0500.
Phone: 1-800-831-4190 • Fax: 1-712-644-2392

Paperback ISBN 0-7891-5493-5
Cover Craft® ISBN 0-7569-0247-9
2 3 4 5 6 7 PP 08 07 06 05 04 03

TABLE of CONTENTS

▼▼▼▼▼▼▼▼▼▼▼

Introduction 4

1. Pepa's Story 9

2. All About Pepa 14

3. Getting Ahead 18

4. Sugar Beet Blues 23

5. Too Cold to Count 27

6. American Girls 32

7. Meanwhile, Back in Milwaukee . . 38

8. A Crying Shame 42

9. Amá's Choice 46

10. Surprises 48

11. Isabel's Fiesta 50

Glossary 54

INTRODUCTION

▼▼▼▼▼▼▼▼▼▼▼

Mexico in 1920

At the beginning of the 20th century, General Porfirio Díaz was in power. He was a **dictator**. This meant that he controlled the money and the power in Mexico.

The common people were tired of the **dictatorship**. They wanted more voice in their government.

Francisco Madero wanted a **democratic** government where the people would share the power. When Díaz saw to it that Madero would not be elected president of Mexico, the Mexican Revolution started.

The date was November 20, 1910, and all over Mexico people took up arms against the government. They were led by such people as Pancho Villa and Emiliano Zapata.

In 1911, Díaz was defeated. He

escaped to France. Madero became president of Mexico. But in 1913, Madero was killed. For the next seven years, the fighting continued in Mexico.

Finally in 1920, a new president, Alvaro Obregón, came into power. The revolution ended.

From 1910 to 1920, many Mexican people fled to the United States. They left for the same reasons that others rebelled. They wanted freedom. They wanted to be safe. And they wanted to earn enough money to live a good life.

UNITED STATES IN 1920

In 1920, the United States had just come out of war and fighting too. In 1916, Pancho Villa had brought the Mexican Revolution to New Mexico and along the United States-Mexican border. President Wilson had sent 12,000 men to fight in Mexico.

Then in 1917, the United States joined with France and England to fight Germany. They were called the Allies, and the war was World War I. By the end of 1918, that war was over. The Allies had won.

The 18th Amendment to the Constitution was passed in 1919. It made making, selling, and shipping alcohol illegal.

The 19th Amendment was passed in 1920. It gave women the right to vote.

By 1920, a new age was beginning. It was the age of fads, Hollywood, and dancing. It was called the Roaring Twenties.

For the first time, more people lived in cities than on farms. Jazz was the popular music. People were driving cars. They were going to the movies. Some were going to **speakeasies** where they drank illegal alcohol.

During this time, women began to wear short hair and short skirts. Some even wore makeup. These women were called *flappers*.

In 1920, Warren G. Harding was president. He died in 1923, and his vice president, Calvin Coolidge, took office.

COMING to AMERICA from MEXICO—1920

1
PEPA'S STORY

This is the story of me. This is why I am writing it.

1. My teacher asked me to.
2. It will help others understand me.
3. It will help me learn about myself.

I will start as far back as I can remember.

I used to live in Mexico. We lived on a **rancho**. It seemed big then. But **Amá** says it was not so big.

I remember my **abuela** singing to me. She sang baby songs. Her voice was soft and sweet. I can still sing some of the songs. I sing them to my doll.

I remember the chickens in the yard. They would scritch-scratch at the dirt.

Once I tried to catch one. I wanted to make it my baby. I didn't have a doll yet. I picked up the chicken. It scratched my cheek. I still have a fine scar.

I remember our house. When I came in from playing outside, I was hot and sweaty. I would sit on the floor in the doorway. I'd put my hot back against the cool wall. A breeze would blow through the doorway. It cooled me off.

I loved my life in Mexico. But things changed. Pancho Villa was on a **rampage**. It wasn't safe to stay there. I'm told we left quickly. I don't remember.

I was five when my family came here in early 1920. "Here" is San Antonio, Texas.

I do remember the train ride. I thought it would be exciting. But it was not. It was long and boring. It was also dirty and smelly.

Amá brought apples. We ate apples for two days. I could do three things on the train.

1. Look out the window.
2. Sleep.
3. Eat apples.

I couldn't look at an apple for a long time after that.

Finally, we arrived in the United States. Amá, **Apá**, and Abuela had to take a test to show how smart they were. If they weren't smart enough, we'd have to go home. Lucky for us, they're smart. And lucky for us, the test was in Spanish!

Then a nurse checked our health. If we were sick, we'd have to go home. Lucky for us, we were healthy.

Then Apá had to pay an $8 tax for each of us. That was $48! Too bad we weren't rich. The $48 paid for Apá, Amá, Abuela, Isabel, Paco, and me.

The money Apá had saved was almost gone. But we didn't care. We were in the United States. We thought that soon we would be rich.

At the time, Isabel was twelve and Paco was eight. I already told you I was five. That was almost five years ago. Half my life. Now I'm ten.

We had family in San Antonio. **Tía** María was very strict. I tried to stay out of her way. **Tío** Leo was fun. I liked it when he joked with me. I had eight cousins. They were María, Manuel, Juan, Jósefa, Ricardo, José, Felipe, and Carlita. And they were all older than I was. They treated me like a baby. I tried to stay out of their way too.

It was very crowded at Tía María and Tío Leo's. We planned to stay with them until Apá **got his feet on the ground.** We would stay just until we could get a place of our own.

First Apá found a job fixing the railroad. The work was very hard. And Apá already had a bad back. That job didn't last too long. Then Apá picked cotton. That was better. But the work only lasted part of the year.

It was a long, long time before Apá would get his feet on the ground.

2
ALL ABOUT PEPA

Now, I will write about me. My name is Pepa Ruíz. My real name is longer. I like my short name better. I already wrote that I am ten years old. I am in the fourth grade at Bell Elementary School. I'm very glad to be in school. You'll understand why later.

I go to San José Church. I sing in the children's choir. I am a very good singer.

I love to sing and dance. I like to put on shows for my family. I've been told that I talk too much. That's one reason I'm writing this. My teacher said anyone who has so much to say should put it down on paper.

I have long brown hair. I can almost sit on it. I wear it in one or two braids. I have big brown eyes. I am a little bit thin. Even so, I have round cheeks.

I want a dog. But Apá says not now—maybe someday.

My very best friend is Lucinda. Lucinda sings prettily too. We like to sing together. I sing the high part. Lucinda sings the **harmony**. We will be famous when we grow up.

I like living in the United States. But I hated it when I was five. And when I was six. And seven. And eight. By nine, I was getting used to it. Now I love it.

I didn't go to school when we first arrived here. But the next year, I did.

At first, I hated school. There are two reasons.

1. I was a little kid. I'd never been away from Amá or Abuela.
2. I didn't speak English.

Amá and Apá spoke Spanish at home. Isabel and Paco were learning English too. But they didn't teach me any words. And my teacher spoke only English. How was I to learn?

That first year was very hard. Words didn't make sense.

I learned by watching. I copied what other kids said. Sometimes I didn't know what I was saying.

Lucinda didn't speak English either then. That made it easier. I could speak Spanish to Lucinda. Together, we tried to figure out things.

The teacher didn't like it when we talked Spanish together. It was against her rules. We had to sneak. We talked to each other on the playground. We walked to school together. We ate lunch together. When the teacher wasn't looking, we spoke Spanish. We used very quiet voices. This is what made Lucinda my very best friend. We didn't have anybody else to talk to. And then, we learned English together.

It took a long time. But little by little, English began to make sense. Now I speak English and Spanish. So do Lucinda, Paco, and Isabel. Amá and Abuela still don't speak much English. Apá had to learn some English for his work.

So at home, we speak only Spanish. At school, I speak only English. Sometimes I feel like two different people.

3
GETTING AHEAD

For a long time, we lived with Tía María and Tío Leo. Amá and Abuela helped Tía María cook. They worked in the garden. They helped take care of the house. We all ate together. But our families slept in separate rooms. In our room, Amá and Apá slept in a bed. Isabel, Paco, and I slept on mats on the floor. Abuela slept with the cousins. That's all the room Tía María and Tío Leo could spare.

Then Apá found a way to get ahead.

"The whole family will have to help," Apá said. "We will all have to work very hard. But it will mean that we can finally get our own place."

We all smiled. We agreed to work hard. Apá didn't tell us what the work would be. Maybe we should have asked.

A few days later, we found out. School was almost out for the summer. Amá and Tía María were fixing supper. Abuela, Isabel, Paco, two cousins, and I sat at the table. Abuela was patting out tortillas. Isabel was doing homework. I was singing. Paco and the cousins were waiting for food.

Apá burst into the kitchen.

"We're leaving for Iowa tonight!" he said.

"Iowa?" we said. "What's Iowa?"

"It's where the work is!" Apá said. "We have to leave soon. Hurry!"

"What about school?" Isabel asked.

"You will only miss a couple of weeks," Apá said. "Next year, we will be back here. You won't even know you missed any school."

"What about me?" Abuela asked.

"You will stay with María," Apá said. He gave Abuela a hug. "We will see you next fall. Then we will be rich. We will get our own place."

Tía María nodded. Abuela nodded too. But she had tears in her eyes.

Isabel looked at Apá. She had daggers in her eyes. But Apá was busy. He didn't notice.

We ate quickly. Apá said there wouldn't be room to bring much along. We didn't have much anyway. Amá packed a little food. Oranges this time.

"They keep well," Amá said.

We said good-bye to Tía María, Abuela, and Tío Leo. But I didn't get to tell Lucinda good-bye. Then we carried our bundles to San José Church.

Soon the truck came. Apá tossed our bundles in the back. Then we all climbed into the back. **Señor** Gonzales and his sons, Juan and José, moved over so we could all squeeze in. Juan was the same age as Isabel. José was a year older than Paco. Another family, the Garcias, came too. They had six kids. All of them were older than me. Again, I was the baby.

The truck was very crowded. We could only sit down when some people stood up.

Apá, Paco, and Amá said hello to everyone. I smiled. Isabel moved to a corner with her back to us all. She rode like that all the way to Iowa.

The trip to Iowa was longer than the train trip from Mexico. It was even more boring. It was bumpier. It was smellier. And, of course, there were oranges.

Some nights, we drove all night. But some nights, we stopped along the way. That part was the best. I picked wildflowers. We had campfires. We sang around the fire. At one place, there was a lake. I went wading.

But every morning, we packed up. We climbed back in the truck. We sat through another long, boring day. I tried to stay awake when we stopped. That way I could sleep all day on the truck.

There was one other good thing about the trip. Because I was the baby, I received special treatment. I got to sit by Amá. Resting against her, I always fell asleep.

I slept most of the way to Iowa. Good thing, because I sure didn't get much rest once we got there.

4
SUGAR BEET BLUES

Things got worse when we arrived in Iowa. We shared a one-room, dirt-floor shack with the Gonzales family. **Señora** Gonzales had stayed in San Antonio with her sick mother. Paco, Isabel, and I shared a single bed. It was a thin mat on the dirt floor. We rolled it up during the day.

At first, only Apá, Isabel, and Paco worked. Amá stayed home with me. She cooked for everyone. I liked that part of the summer best. I helped her.

Sometimes Amá would play with me. I'd be the Amá, and she'd be the little one. She always wanted me to carry her. I would try, but I couldn't pick her up! We would always end up laughing.

By late summer, there was more work. Amá and I went into the fields too. We picked tomatoes and melons. Amá picked most of them. I brought water. And I got Amá a new basket when hers was full.

Sometimes I helped Isabel, Paco, or Apá too.

The best part about picking melons was eating them. I just sat down in the dirt and cracked the melon. I dug out the seeds with my hands. Then I enjoyed the sweet treat.

Of course, I didn't earn money while I was eating. And I was all sticky. Dirt stuck to me. Bugs liked me better too. But it was worth it.

Amá and Isabel didn't have an easy time. They had to do more work than anyone. They worked in the fields all day. They worked from early morning until it was almost dark. They were very tired. But at the end of the day, they still had to fix supper for everyone. That's just the way it was.

After supper, it was time for bed. Then the first thing I knew, it was time to get up again.

And so the summer went.

Soon it was time to go back to school. But Apá had heard about sugar beets—in Wisconsin.

"What's Wisconsin?" we all asked.

"It's another state. Just over the river and up the road," Apá said.

"Sugar beets ripen in October," he went on.

"If we just work this one season, we can go back to San Antonio this winter," Apá promised.

Isabel wanted to go back now. Paco didn't care. He didn't like school much anyway. None of us knew English very well yet. But we sure weren't going to learn it in the sugar beet fields.

Apá said it didn't matter what Isabel wanted. We were going to Wisconsin. Again, he didn't see the daggers in her eyes.

So fall came. We moved to Wisconsin. The Gonzales family moved with us.

At least the new shack had two rooms and a wood floor.

Working in the sugar beet fields was hard. You had to bend lower. You had to pull and dig. And Amá and Isabel still had to feed everyone at night.

Isabel grew quieter and quieter. Nobody seemed to notice but me. Everyone else was too tired.

5
TOO COLD TO COUNT

Finally the sugar beet harvest was almost done. Apá had some news one night.

"I can get a good job here," he said.

We all looked at him.

"What kind of job?" Amá asked.

"The **tannery** in town needs workers," Apá said. "I'm going to work there. We will stay here one year. I will earn good money. We can save. Then we can go back to San Antonio. Or maybe Mexico. It's safer now. We will buy a house."

"But Apá . . ." Isabel said.

"My mind is made up," Apá said. "We will stay here through next summer. This is the best thing for our family."

Apá turned and walked away. I saw the daggers in Isabel's eyes again. Why couldn't anyone else see them?

So we stayed in Wisconsin after the sugar beet harvest. We moved to a small house in town. It wasn't any better than the sugar beet shack. But the Gonzales family had gone back to San Antonio. It was just our family again.

Isabel went to high school. She was 14. Paco and I went to a grade school.

My teacher was Mrs. Johnson. She said, "Now you have a chance to make something of yourself."

I wasn't sure what she meant. I tried very hard. I drew lots of pictures of me. She seemed to like them.

By then, it was late November. We had never felt such cold. It cut through our clothes. We all had bad colds. We sneezed and sneezed. We kept one another awake all night.

The house was cold too. We had to buy coal to heat it. It was dirty and smelly. We'd never used it before. We hated the coal. And we hated the cold.

When we woke up in the morning, a fire had to be started in the stove. Apá or Paco would jump out of bed and start the fire. Then, slowly, the house would heat up.

Apá hadn't planned on spending money for coal. "Now," he said, "it will take longer. We might have to stay in Wisconsin another year."

It was still November. We didn't know that it would get even colder.

We only had cotton clothes. In Mexico and San Antonio, we didn't need many warm clothes. We didn't have warm coats. And we only had sandals for shoes. We ran all the way to school just to keep warm. It didn't work very well. We were still cold.

Every Sunday, we went to church. The church was called Our Lady of Constant Care. Amá got us coats and real shoes from the church. The clothes had belonged to other people. When they were through with their clothes, they gave them to the church. Amá got coats for everyone.

My coat was brown wool. It was too big. It dragged on the ground. I didn't like getting it dirty. But how nice it was to be warm! I wanted to wear my coat all the time.

My shoes were big too. But they covered my toes. I wore rags around my feet. They helped fill the shoes. And they helped keep me warm.

Apá didn't like what Amá had done.
He said it was **charity**. At first he said
we must take the coats back. Apá was
proud. But Apá was sad too. He didn't
have money to buy coats or shoes and
still save enough to get us back to San
Antonio.

Apá let us keep the coats and shoes.
Good thing he did because we needed
them badly.

Then December came. It was even
colder. Apá let Amá get us free knit
hats and mittens. I don't know what we
would have done without Our Lady of
Constant Care. Still, the cold hurt.

But just being cold wasn't enough.
Then the snow came. It was
beautiful—white and sparkly. And each
big snowflake made a lacy design.

But the snow was cold. I hated it. It
froze my feet. And it was slick. I can't
tell you how many times I fell down.

6
AMERICAN GIRLS

Many Mexicans worked at the
tanneries. We all lived in the same part
of Milwaukee. It was called the **barrio**.
Amá made an **altar** in the house.

She lit candles and said prayers for us and for our faraway family. I could tell Amá missed Abuela and our family in Mexico. But we had to go where Apá went.

At Christmas, our church had **las posadas**. Paco played Joseph. We followed him and Mary around the neighborhood. Amá and Apá were very proud of Paco.

For Christmas, I received a doll. I think the ladies at Our Lady of Constant Care gave her to me. I named her Jean. She had blond hair and blue eyes.

I was trying hard to be a good American. I was trying to learn English. But I didn't look like Jean.

It was hard for me to feel like an American. Everyone around me was Mexican. Yes, I was learning a little English at school. But I didn't know much about how Americans lived.

▼▼▼▼▼▼▼▼▼▼

My birthday was three days after Christmas. For my birthday, Apá took us to a movie. None of us had ever been to a movie before. We saw Charlie Chaplin. He was a funny little man with a mustache. He wore a funny little hat. He carried a cane, and he walked funny. His eyes got very big sometimes.

A piano played music. But the movie was silent. When someone in the movie talked, the words were printed on the screen. We didn't know what the words said.

After the movie, I thought that American men must be like Charlie Chaplin. I looked for men who walked funny and carried canes.

Isabel was learning more about Americans. She went to a school that had all kinds of kids. Isabel even made friends with an American girl, Maxine.

Maxine was Isabel's best friend. She looked like my doll Jean. Maxine had blond hair and blue eyes. Isabel and I wanted to look like that.

Isabel and Maxine didn't seem like they

would be friends. They looked so very
different. Isabel had long black hair. She
wore it in a braid down her back. She
wore long, Mexican skirts. Maxine wore
plaid dresses. She wore her hair pulled
back. But it hung loose down her back.

I guess on the inside, Maxine and
Isabel were more alike.

On New Year's Eve, Maxine asked
Isabel to spend the night at her house.
Amá and Apá said yes.

When Isabel came home, it was like
the world had ended. I'd never heard so
much screaming and yelling. Isabel's long
black braid was gone. She and Maxine
had given themselves **bobs**. Now Isabel's
hair barely covered her ears.

Amá and Apá were *fit to be tied*. That
meant they were really mad. They made
Isabel sit in a corner. They told Isabel
that she could never go to Maxine's again.
In fact, she could never see Maxine again.
She couldn't even speak to her. They said
she would have to let her hair grow out.
And she would have to wear a scarf on
her head until it did.

Isabel cried all day.

"How unfair they are!" she cried to me. "American girls can wear short hair. Aren't I an American girl now?"

She didn't dare say that to Apá.

Later, Apá tried to talk to us all. "Mexican girls are good girls," he said. "They don't cut their hair. They don't act like flappers."

Isabel didn't talk back to Apá. In fact, she didn't talk to Apá at all. He thought she was showing respect. But I knew how mad she was.

A few days later, Maxine invited Isabel over after school. Isabel didn't ask if she could go. She knew what the answer would be. She just went.

When she came home, Apá was waiting for her. He had a look on his face like I'd never seen before. I don't ever want to make Apá look like that. He took Isabel into the bedroom. I could hear her crying.

The next day, Isabel didn't go to school. She was on the train to San Antonio. She was going back to live

with Abuela and Tía María. They
would take care of her. Isabel wouldn't
be able to go anywhere without Tía
María, who was very strict.

7

MEANWHILE, BACK IN MILWAUKEE

I found out later that Apá used part of our savings to buy a train ticket for Isabel. He had someone at work make a sign for her. He hung it on a string around her neck. It said: Isabel Ruíz. Do not talk to me. Deliver to Leo Ruíz in San Antonio, Texas.

Isabel said it was horrible. She was 14 years old. She almost looked like a grown-up. And Apá had hung a sign around her neck as if she were a small child. Of course, as soon as the train pulled out of the station, Isabel took it off. Then she threw it out the window. Good thing Apá didn't walk along the tracks. If so, Isabel would be living with the nuns now.

I missed Isabel. And I missed Abuela. I didn't like having our family apart. Amá was sad too. I think that Apá and Paco were also sad. I hugged my doll Jean.

Paco and I were as good as gold. It's not that we didn't want to go back to San Antonio. It's not that we didn't want to see Isabel. But it felt like our family was falling apart. We wanted to stay with Amá and Apá. For that reason, we wanted to stay in Milwaukee.

Paco and I both hated winter. Color was gone from everything. Gray was everywhere.

Sometimes, we slid on the ice. Sometimes, our feet got stuck in the gooey mud. Other kids enjoyed the ice and mud. Not us!

But we were getting used to our school. We were making friends.

Apá liked his job. It was messy and smelly. But it didn't seem to hurt his back.

Apá stained the leather. Some days, he came home black. Some days, he was red. Some days, he was brown. He even came home yellow. We always waited to see what color Apá would be. The dye didn't wash off. So after a while, Apá's hands and arms were very dark brown. They are still that way.

One day turned into the next for us. Our hearts were sad for Isabel. And for Abuela. But life was going on without them. English was becoming easier.

More mud than ice was underfoot now. Color returned. The grass became green. The trees began to bloom. Spring flowers bloomed too. Easter came and went.

"Soon it will be time to go back to the fields," Apá said.

We all looked at him. How Apá could just turn our lives around!

"What about your job at the tannery?" Amá asked.

"I can get it back next winter," Apá said. "We can make more money if we all work in the fields."

"What about Isabel?" I asked.

"Isabel is fine," Apá said. "Abuela, Tía María, and Tío Leo are taking good care of her."

Again, Paco and I missed the end of school. Again, we didn't get to say good-bye to our friends. Again, we headed for the fields.

We moved back into the one-room, dirt-floor shack with the Gonzales family.

8

A CRYING SHAME

It's a shame Isabel couldn't be with us. I think she would have been happy to plant tomatoes. She would have liked to hoe weeds. She would have smiled at each tomato she picked. But Apá said we couldn't afford to bring her back. She would just have to stay in San Antonio.

Now that I was eight, I was more help. Sometimes I went down the row with Amá. Sometimes with Apá. Sometimes with Paco. They let me bring them water. They let me pull weeds. I even picked. Sometimes I ate a small tomato. By the end of summer, I had my own basket to fill.

Because I was working more, that summer was harder than the one before. Amá and I had no time to be alone. We didn't get to play house. And now that Isabel was gone, I had to help Amá cook.

I grew up a lot that summer. At eight and a half, I was doing work that the women usually did.

When school started in the fall, Paco and I didn't go. We worked in the melon fields.

Then we moved back to the sugar beet shack.

I didn't work in the sugar beet fields. I wasn't strong enough. But Amá did. Sometimes I went with Amá. I helped with what I could. Sometimes I fixed supper all by myself.

We lived too far away from the school for the **migrants**. So I couldn't go to school. I wondered why it was called the migrant school. I went there when I wasn't a migrant. And now that I was one, I couldn't go.

Amá wasn't feeling very well. She didn't say so, but I could tell. Her face was looking old. Her hands were stiff. She didn't stand as tall as before. I think her back ached. But every day, she went to the fields. Then she came home and cooked.

Some of our life in the fields was hard. It made even a strong person tired. Nights were short. Days were long.

We had one day off a week. That was Sunday. It was the day to do the wash, buy the food, and do everything that didn't get done during the week. It was supposed to be a day of rest. But there was too much to do.

We did have some fun though. We sang songs. We laughed. We talked about the day we would see Abuela,

Isabel, Tía María, and Tío Leo again.

Before long, the days got short. It began to get cold. Sugar beet time was almost over. It was time to go back to Milwaukee. Apá would go back to the tannery.

Paco and I were excited. We would go back to school. We'd see our friends from last year. Amá could stay home. She would only take care of us and the house.

Then Apá had more news.

9
Amá's Choice

"We have a choice," Apá said.

"The Gonzales family is going back to San Antonio soon. There is room on the truck for us. We can go with them. Or we can stay in Milwaukee."

I held my breath.

"What do you think?" Apá asked Amá.

"San Antonio," Amá said. She had tears in her eyes.

"Good," Apá said. "Then we will go back to San Antonio."

I still held my breath.

"I don't have a job there," Apá said. "But a tannery is there. Perhaps they will hire me."

I still held my breath.

"If they don't hire me," Apá said, "I will find something else."

I still held my breath.

"What's the matter, Pepa?" Apá asked. "You're turning blue."

"Whew!" I let out my breath.

"I was afraid you'd change your mind," I said.

"No," Apá said. "If Amá wants to go back to San Antonio, then we go."

Paco and I began to laugh. Amá began to cry. Apá looked at us all. He just shook his head.

Two days later, we were back in the truck. Again, we stopped and had campfires. Again, I picked wildflowers. But this time, I didn't sleep too much. I watched the countryside roll by. The beautiful American countryside.

10
SURPRISES

Isabel was waiting for us at San
José Church. I jumped out of the truck
and ran to her. She picked me up. She
twirled me around. Amá, Apá, and
Paco came running.

Everyone got a big hug.

"Your hair looks pretty, **m'ija**," Apá said. Isabel's hair hung down past her shoulders.

"**Gracias**, Apá," she said. She looked at him. There were no daggers in her eyes this time.

Apá and Paco took our belongings off the wagon. Tía María, Abuela, and Tío Leo ran up. Everyone got another hug.

"I have a surprise for you," Isabel said to me.

I jumped up and down. "What?" I asked.

Isabel took my hand. "Come here," she said. She led me across the churchyard.

Some children were playing. One girl came forward.

"Lucinda!" I cried. I ran and hugged my friend. Lucinda hugged me back. Then she looked at me.

"You've grown so!" she said.

I laughed. "Your English is good."

"Yours too," Lucinda said. "Shall we speak Spanish now?"

"I have a better idea," I said. "Let's learn French next!"

11
ISABEL'S FIESTA

We stayed at Tía María and Tío Leo's while Apá looked for a job. When Apá took a job at the tannery, we looked for a place to live.

We found a nice little house. We live there now. It has three rooms and a porch. A live oak tree grows in the backyard. Amá and Abuela have planted a garden. But no one will have to work in this garden all day, every day, all summer long.

Our house is near Tía María's. I go to my old school. It's the one I went to before I knew English. And it's the one Lucinda goes to. This is why I'm glad to be in school.

Now I know what my teacher in Wisconsin meant. The way to make something of myself is to stay in school. I must keep learning new things.

▼▼▼▼▼▼▼▼▼▼

Soon after we moved back to San Antonio, Isabel had a birthday. She turned 15. This is a very important birthday for a Mexican girl. It is called her **quinceañera**.

Amá and Apá planned a big party at the church. Isabel got to invite all of her friends.

Abuela, Tía María, and Amá made Isabel a new white dress. They baked many treats for the party.

On the night of the party, Isabel looked beautiful. She had on her long white dress. She wore her hair piled on top of her head. She wore a little crown of flowers. She was the queen of the party. It was almost better than being a bride. She didn't have to share the limelight with anyone. Not even a groom.

I can't wait until I'm 15. But I guess I'll have to.

Having a big sister is good. I've learned some important things from Isabel.

1. Don't cut your hair. It makes Apá very upset.
2. You can have American friends. Apá has said it's okay. Just don't act like a flapper.

Now San Antonio feels like home. Iowa and Wisconsin had their good points. But it was too cold there. And it was too far away from family.

Now I love being an American. And I love being Mexican. This is the third thing I learned from Isabel.

3. If you play your cards right, you can pretty much have it all.

That's what I want. I want to be Mexican. And I want to be American. I want to have it all.

Glossary

abuela Spanish word for "grandmother"

altar table that serves as a center of worship

amá old-fashioned Spanish term for "mother"

apá old-fashioned Spanish term for "father"

barrio neighborhood of Spanish-speaking people

bob short haircut

charity aid given to those in need

democratic having all people rule either directly or indirectly

dictator person with absolute power

dictatorship government ruled by one person or a small group

flappers	young women of the early 20th century who did not follow what was considered proper conduct
get one's feet on the ground	to get steady employment with earnings enough to support one's self and a family
gracias	Spanish word for "thank you"
harmony	combination of different musical notes sung or played at the same time
las posadas	pre-Christmas celebration
migrant	person who moves from place to place in order to find work
m'ija	Spanish word for "my daughter"

quinceañera Spanish word for a girl's "fifteenth" birthday, which is celebrated with a special party

rampage violent action or riot

rancho Spanish word for "small ranch"

señor Spanish word for "mister"

señora Spanish word for "mistress" or "madam"

speakeasy club or place where alcoholic beverages were sold illegally

tannery place where animal hides are treated and turned into leather

tía Spanish word for "aunt"

tío Spanish word for "uncle"